The Thai Cave Rescue

Jill McDougall

Contents

Author's Note

This text is a historical recount based on real events that took place in Thailand in 2018.

A Great Adventure

Saturday, 23 June 2018

On a sunny morning in northern Thailand, 12 boys on the Wild Boar soccer team were feeling excited. After soccer practice, their coach, Ekkapol Chantawong (known as Coach Eak), was taking them to explore the Tham Luang (pronounced *tam loo-ong*) caves, not far from their village.

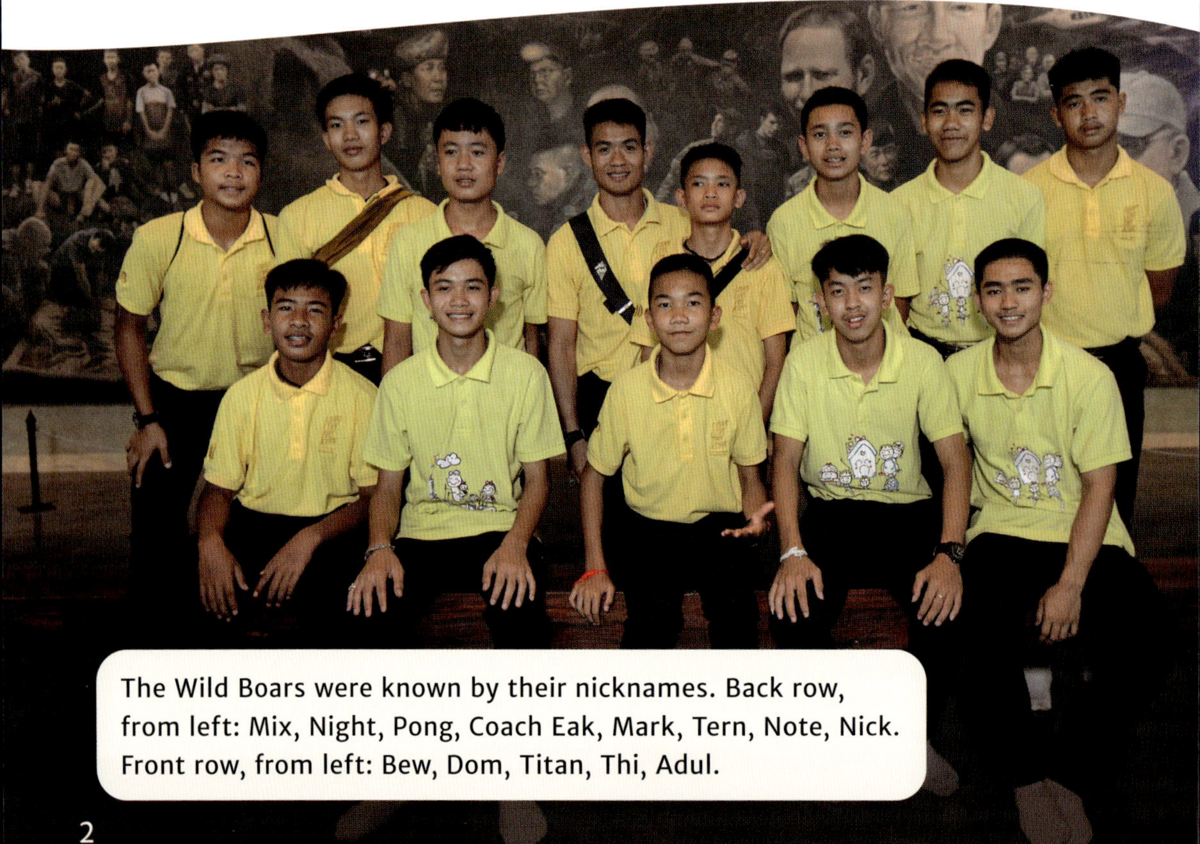

The Wild Boars were known by their nicknames. Back row, from left: Mix, Night, Pong, Coach Eak, Mark, Tern, Note, Nick. Front row, from left: Bew, Dom, Titan, Thi, Adul.

The Tham Luang caves stretch for over ten kilometres underneath the Doi Nang Non mountain range. The caves are made up of large **chambers**, winding passages and narrow tunnels. The biggest chambers were given names such as "Underwater World" and "Hidden City" by some of the boys. For them, this trip was going to be a great adventure.

After stopping for a quick snack at a food stall, the Wild Boars and their coach set off on their bikes. The boys, who were aged from 11 to 16, carried nothing but their backpacks and flashlights.

Location of the Tham Luang Caves in Thailand

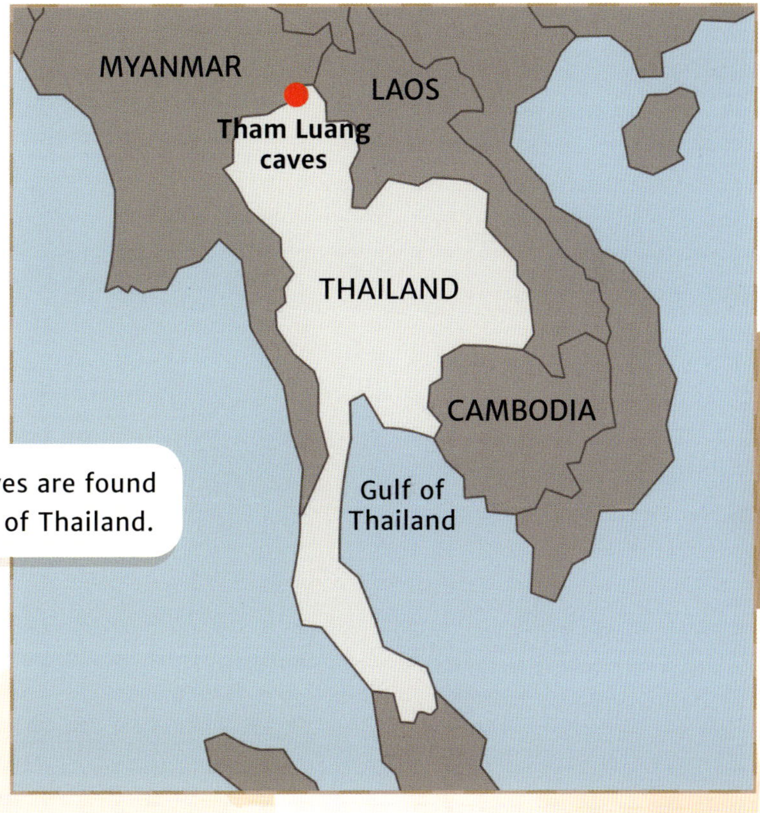

The Tham Luang caves are found in the northern part of Thailand.

As the boys approached the cave entrance, they stopped to bow and pay their respects at a **shrine** decorated with an image of the **Buddha**. Most of the Wild Boar boys were Buddhist, and they believed that the Tham Luang mountains were a **sacred** place.

A shrine to Buddha is outside the entrance of the Tham Luang caves.

Outside the cave was a sign written in Thai and English. One of the boys, Titan (aged 11), paused to read it. The biggest word was "Danger!!" The sign explained that July to November was flooding season.

Titan thought about the warning. It was the end of June, so the dangerous period hadn't started yet. Feeling relieved, he followed the others into the cave.

The air grew cooler as Coach Eak and the boys made their way through the large chambers and twisting tunnels. Overhead hung spiky **stalactites**.

Stalactites form over thousands of years. When water drips from the ceiling of a cave, it leaves behind minerals that harden into hanging cones.

The boys turned left at a junction where three tunnels join, called Sam Yaek, and then continued on, using their flashlights to light the way. As the cave walls began to close in, the boys wriggled through the narrow spaces on their bellies.

After three hours, the boys had travelled around five kilometres. It was time to turn back.

stalactites in the Tham Luang caves

Trapped

Outside the caves, heavy rain had been falling on the mountainside. The **monsoon season** had arrived early.

Soon, water was rushing through the caves, and the boys discovered that the rising flood had blocked their way out. As the swirling water rose higher, the boys were forced to climb onto a small, rocky ledge.

Coach Eak was not very worried. He thought they might be able to swim through the flooded part of the cave. He had some rope with him, so he tied one end around his waist and gave the other end to three of the oldest boys. "If I don't tug the rope, you can swim after me," he told them.

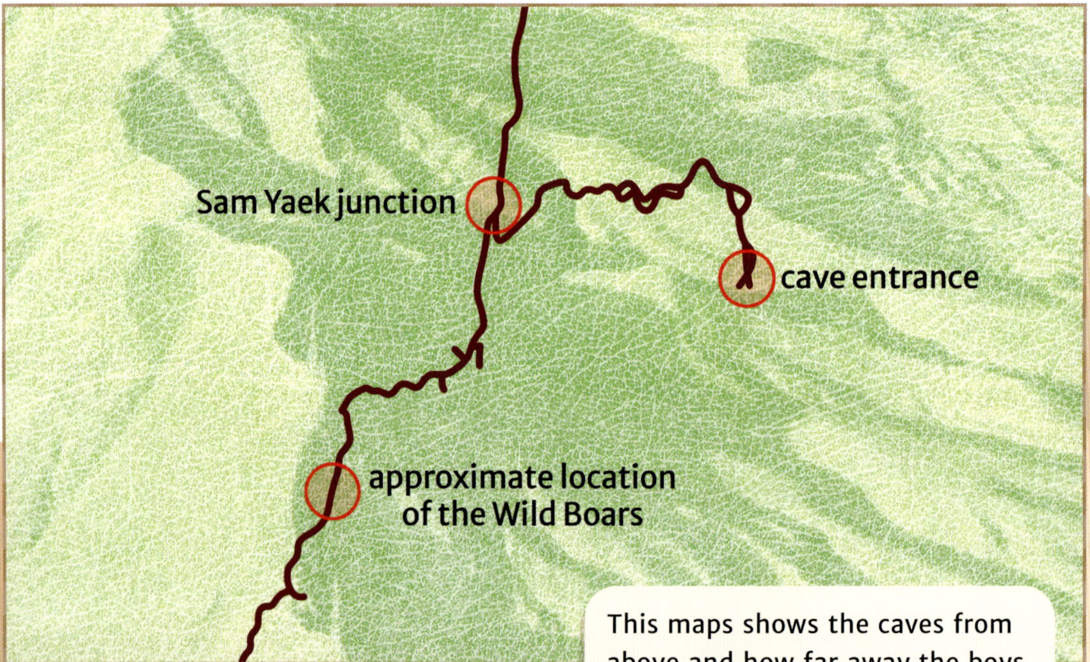

This maps shows the caves from above and how far away the boys were from the entrance.

Coach Eak plunged into the chilly water and swam a few strokes. He soon realised there was no air space above him. The water had reached the ceiling of the flooded part of the cave, and he was running out of breath.

Quickly, Coach Eak yanked on the rope, and the boys pulled him back. “We can’t get out,” he told them. “We must wait until the water level drops.”

In tropical areas of the world, the wet monsoon season brings heavy rains. The season begins when warm winds bring moist air from the ocean to the land.

Rain clouds move quickly over the mountains in northern Thailand during monsoon season.

The Search Begins

Meanwhile, it was getting late, and the boys' families were beginning to worry. Why had the boys not returned home? After sharing frantic messages on **social media**, family members made their way to the caves. Here, they found the boys' bikes and some soccer boots inside the cave entrance. Quickly, the families raised the alarm.

The boys' bicycles were found near the entrance of the cave.

The boys' families prayed outside the cave while they waited for news.

That night, rescue teams from the local area arrived at Tham Luang and began to search the caves. When they arrived at the Sam Yaek junction, they found the boys' footprints and some backpacks. But beyond the junction, the passages were flooded with rushing water.

The next morning, Thai soldiers arrived to help with the rescue. They brought in long pipes and water pumps. The soldiers began to pump water out of the caves so the rescue teams could get through. But even as they pumped water out, the rain grew heavier, so the water levels continued to rise.

Rescue teams worked together to carry pipes and pumps up the mountain to try to clear the caves of water.

Monday, 25 June 2018

It continued to rain on the Doi Nang Non mountains, and water poured into the Sam Yaek junction. The **current** had grown so strong that heavy sandbags, which were placed to help stop water from getting in, were being swept out of the caves.

In the early hours of Monday morning, 20 Thai Navy SEALs arrived at Tham Luang to take over the rescue. These men were experienced **scuba divers** who were used to working in dangerous conditions.

"SEAL" is an abbreviation of the words **s**ea, **a**ir and **l**and. Navy SEALs train longer than others in the military, and they learn how to scuba dive and parachute.

When the SEALs attempted to dive past the Sam Yaek junction, they found that the floodwaters were so powerful, they were being carried backwards.

It seemed that the search was going to be harder than anyone had imagined.

Members of the Thai Navy and some volunteers stand in the floodwaters near the entrance to the cave.

Meditation and Prayer

Tuesday, 26 June 2018

The Wild Boars had now been trapped for three days. They shivered in the damp air, and they were so hungry their bellies ached. Coach Eak suggested they drink the cave water flowing past them. It tasted clean, like **spring water**.

The boys kept checking the water that blocked their way, but it wasn't going down. Instead, the flood was rising, and they were forced to move further up the slope.

To help the boys stay calm, Coach Eak led them through meditation exercises. "Let's observe our breath and calm our minds," he told them. The boys sat still in the dark cave and followed their coach's lead, breathing slowly and deeply.

Some of the boys scratched a message into the cave wall: "13 BOYS LOST".

Water flows down the cave walls in Tham Luang, forming a type of crystal over time.

At night, Coach Eak and the boys huddled together on the narrow ledge and chanted a Thai Buddhist prayer. Adul (aged 14), the only **Christian** on the team, found a space to pray, too.

The boys wondered if anybody was coming for them. Little did they know that news was spreading around the world about 12 boys and their coach trapped in a cave.

Ekkapol "Eak" Chantawong, the Wild Boars' soccer coach, had also trained as a monk, where he practised meditation for almost ten years.

The A-Team

Outside Tham Luang, thousands of people had gathered. There were news reporters from around the world, as well as hundreds of rescue volunteers. Food stalls were set up to serve hot noodles and chicken rice to feed everyone.

The families of the boys waited anxiously by the cave entrance. Sometimes, they would call out to the boys, with their voices cracking, "My son, I'm here! I'm waiting for you!"

School friends of the Wild Boars sang songs into the cave to encourage the boys, and classmates folded paper cranes as a symbol of hope for the boys' safe return.

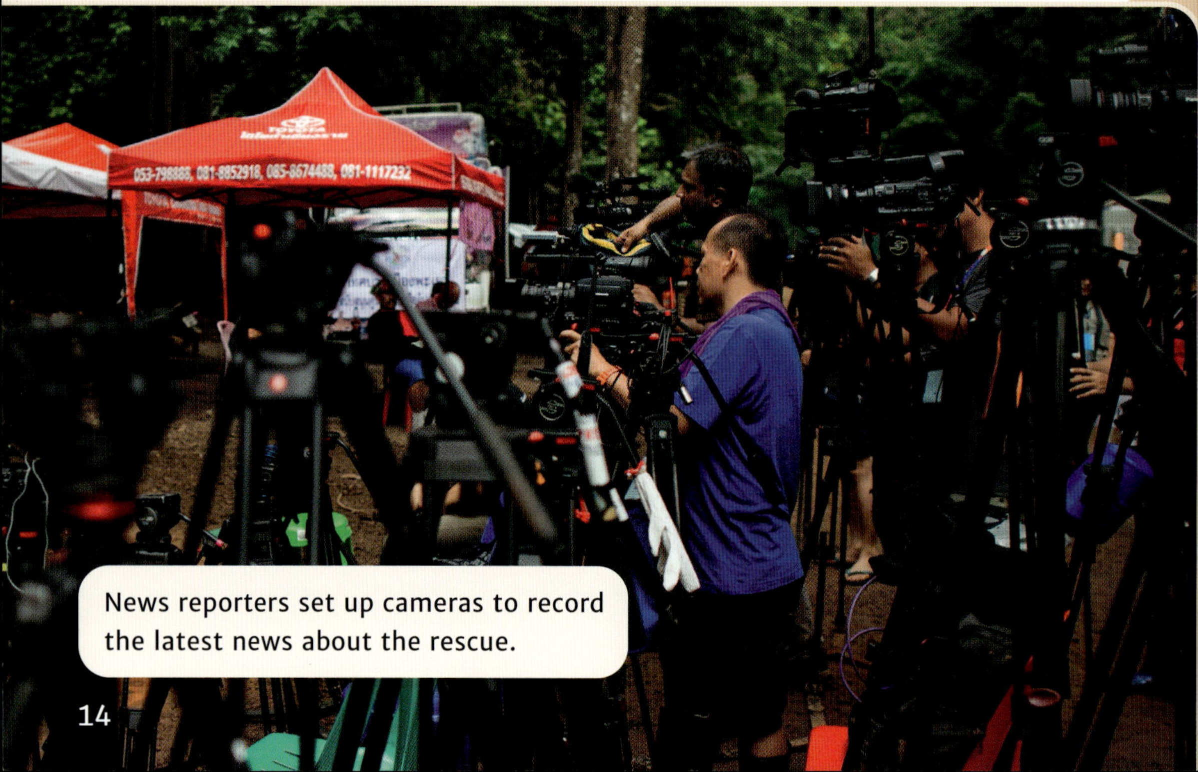

News reporters set up cameras to record the latest news about the rescue.

The Thai government decided to ask some of the world's best cave divers to join the search. Two divers from England quickly agreed to help. These men, Rick Stanton and John Volanthen, were often called the "A-team", as they were experts at rescuing people trapped in caves.

A few days later, Rick and John arrived in Thailand. They started diving right away, making their way through the winding passages of Tham Luang.

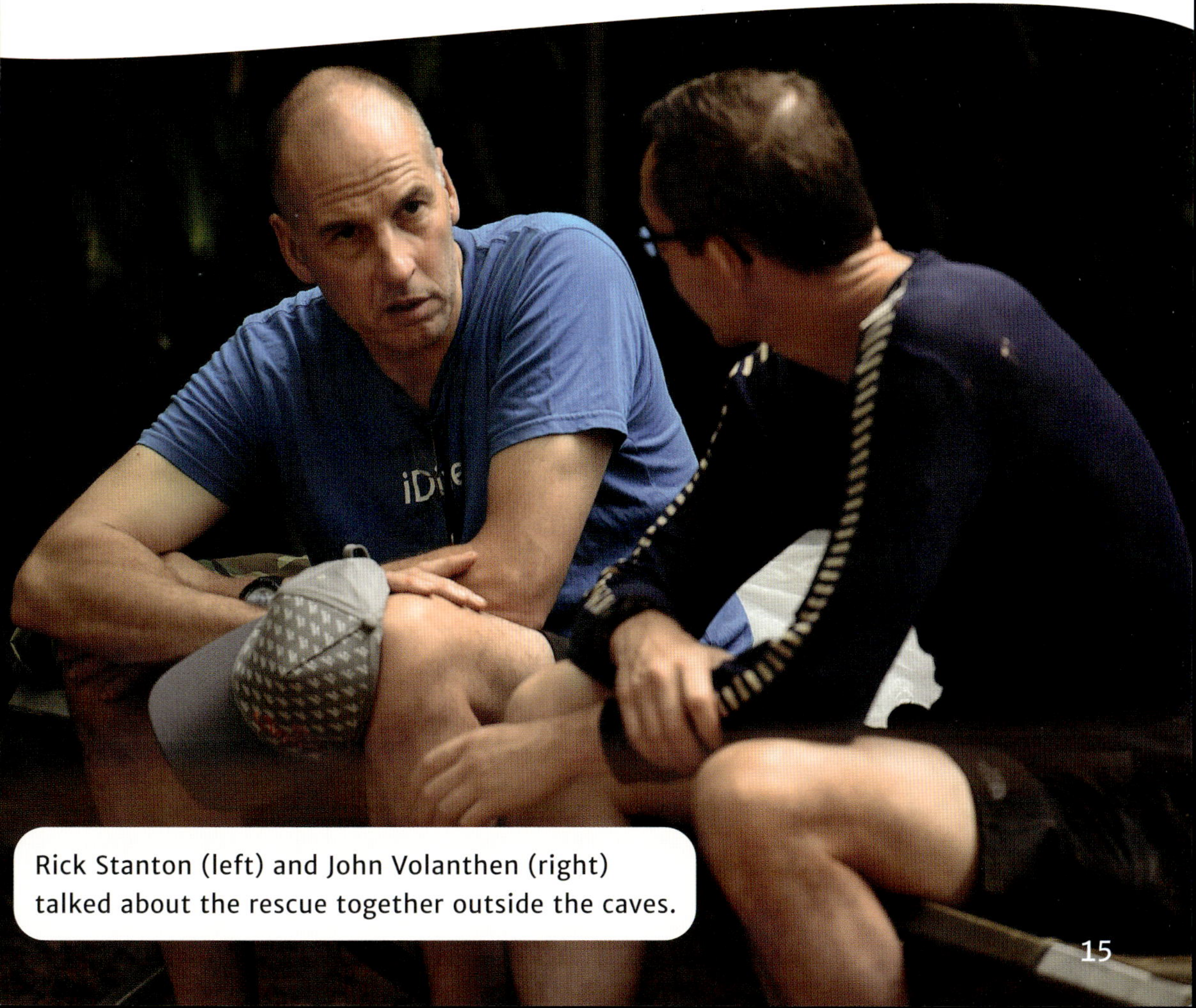

Rick Stanton (left) and John Volanthen (right) talked about the rescue together outside the caves.

Wednesday, 27 June 2018

The English divers soon discovered that there were several dangerous sumps – low areas that fill up with water – in the tunnels of Tham Luang. The sumps had jagged rocks along the walls, and the current was so strong, the divers had to jam their fingers into the mud in order to crawl forward.

Sumps often block access to dry passages beyond them.

John and Rick wore special diving gear every time they dived in the caves.

Before Rick and John reached the Sam Yaek junction, they heard voices! However, it was not the Wild Boars. The divers had found four Thai workers who had been pumping water out of the cave and had become trapped when the floodwaters rose, just like the boys.

One by one, Rick and John pulled the workers through the sumps and back to safety.

The English divers now realised just how bad the conditions were inside Tham Luang. Rescuing the Wild Boars would require all of their courage and skill.

But first, they needed to find them.

People from around the world worked together to plan each dive the rescue workers would make into the caves.

Monday, 2 July 2018

The boys had been trapped inside the mountain for over a week, and no help had arrived. "We must not give up," Coach Eak told them.

In a desperate attempt to save themselves, the boys used rocks to dig tunnels into the base of the cave.

Outside, the monsoon rains had continued to pour down, and the tunnels inside Tham Luang were like raging rivers. For days, the English divers were unable to dive through the caves.

Some of the tunnels the boys dug were almost 4 metres long.

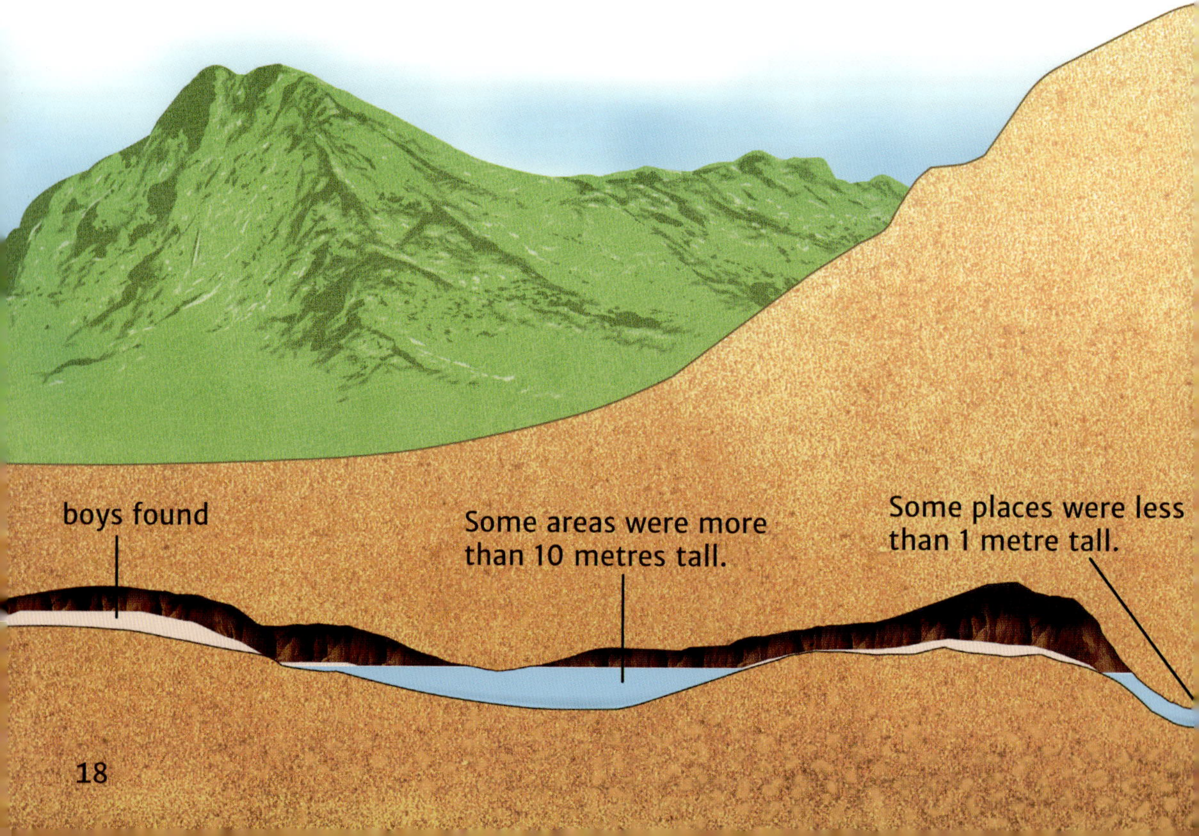

Finally, on Monday morning, the weather cleared. This was the opportunity everyone had been waiting for. Rick and John would make one last effort to find the boys.

As the divers made their way through the muddy sumps, they carried guide ropes that they tied to rocks as they went. These ropes would help them find their way out again.

At last, the divers were able to get through the Sam Yaek junction, and they reached a patch of dry sand on the other side. Here, Rick took off his diving mask and listened. He was stunned when he heard something up ahead.

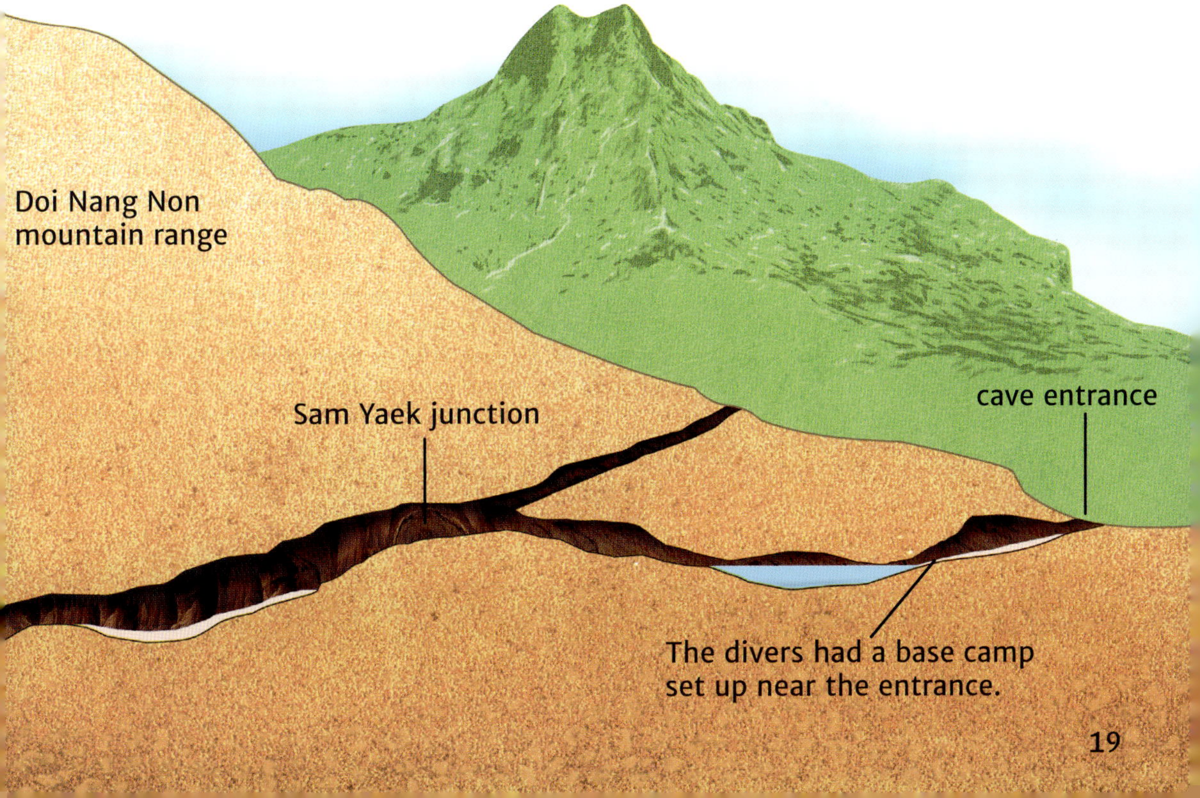

Is Anyone There?

Some of the Wild Boars were digging with rocks when they heard an unexpected sound – a man's voice! The boys froze in the darkness, straining to hear the voice again.

"Is anyone there?" called the man.

Fourteen-year-old Adul moved down the slope as fast as his weak body could carry him. "Hello!" he called back.

"Are you okay?" asked the man.

"Yes," answered Adul. "We are okay."

"How many of you?"

"Thirteen," replied Adul.

"Thirteen? Brilliant," said the man.

The English divers explained that the boys could not be brought out straightaway. However, Thai Navy SEALs would arrive the next day with food and medicine.

"I am very happy," Adul told the divers.

"We are happy, too," replied the English divers, Rick and John.

Adul was one of the few boys who could communicate with the divers in English. The boys who only spoke Thai were desperately trying to understand the conversation.

Soon, the divers disappeared back into the water.

Outside Tham Luang, the news spread quickly to the boys' families and school friends. The boys had been found!

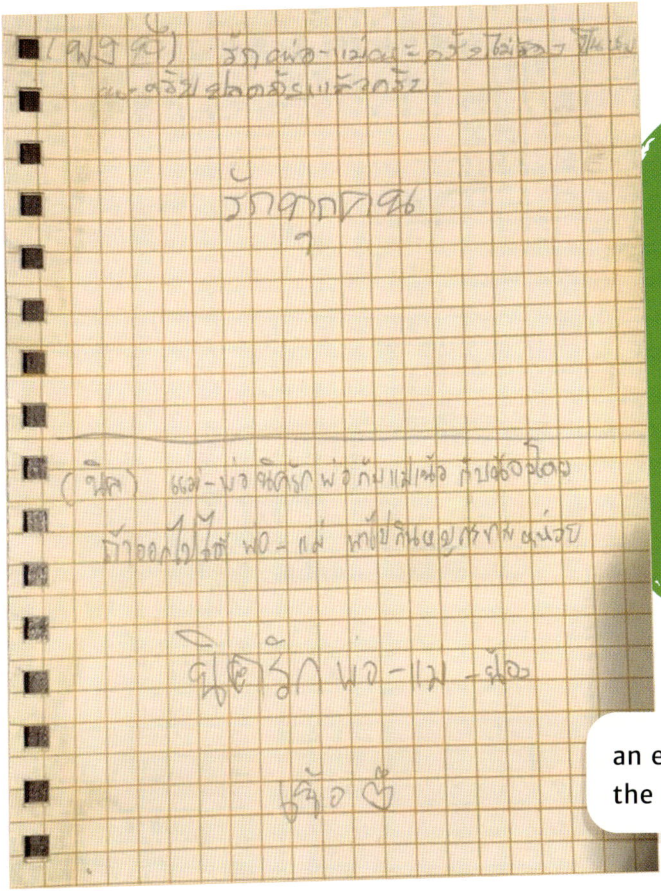

The boys wrote notes to their parents while they were trapped in the cave.

Pong (aged 13) wrote:
I love Dad and Mum. Don't worry about me I'm safe.

Mix (aged 13) wrote:
Don't worry about me, I miss everyone ... The Navy SEALs take care of me very well.

an example of some of the notes the boys wrote to their families

The English divers had taken a video of their meeting with the Wild Boars, and it was posted online. The video was soon watched by millions of people around the world.

Tuesday, 3 July 2018

The next day, some Thai Navy SEALs were able to make their way through the tunnels by crawling and diving to deliver food and supplies to the boys. However, it was not the fried rice and chicken the boys had been dreaming about. Under a doctor's orders, they were put on a special diet of liquid food for a few days.

Four SEALs, including a Navy doctor, stayed in the cave with the Wild Boars. The SEALs played games with the boys, such as checkers, using mud as the pieces.

Despite their polite smiles, the boys were weak and exhausted. The level of **oxygen** in the cave was dropping, and it was clear that the boys needed to be rescued quickly.

the four Navy SEALs who stayed in the cave with the boys

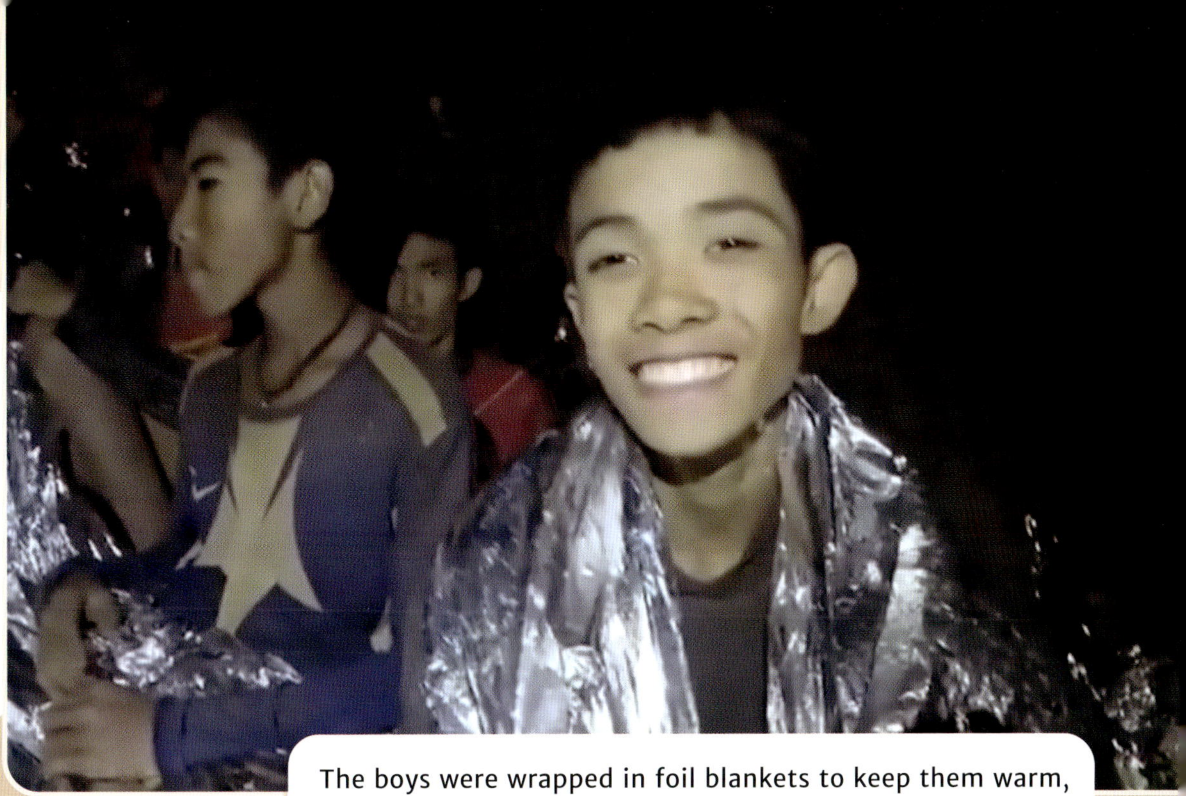

The boys were wrapped in foil blankets to keep them warm, which were brought to them by the Navy SEALs.

Meanwhile, members of the Thai government were holding meetings with experts from different countries to discuss how the boys could be brought out.

Some people suggested that the boys should be trained to scuba dive through the caves. Others wondered about drilling a tunnel from above. A few people thought the Wild Boars might have to stay trapped until the monsoon season was over. But that was at least four months away – how would the boys survive such a terrible wait?

Finally, it was decided that the cave divers would attempt to carry the boys through the winding passages and dangerous sumps.

The Rescue

Sunday, 8 July 2018

Rescue divers from around the world had arrived in Thailand to help carry the boys through the tunnels. Two divers from Australia, Dr Richard Harris and Dr Craig Challen, would play an important role in the rescue.

Dr Craig Challen (left) and Dr Richard Harris (right) standing in front of the cave

The first rescue divers to reach the boys' chamber were greeted with much excitement by the Wild Boars. At last, they would leave the darkness and damp of the cave!

The divers brought a face mask and an air tank with them for each boy. The boys would also wear several wetsuits each to help them stay warm while they were carried through the chilly water.

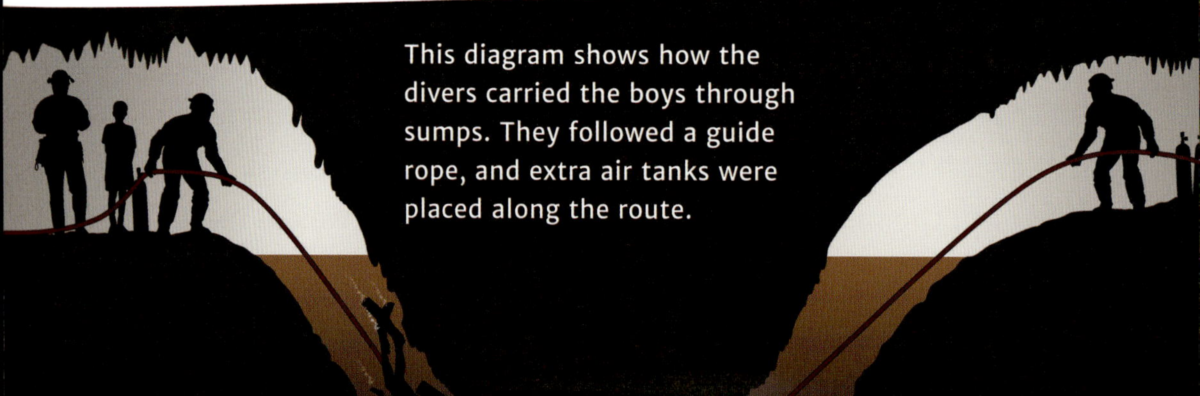

This diagram shows how the divers carried the boys through sumps. They followed a guide rope, and extra air tanks were placed along the route.

The first boy to be rescued was Note (aged 14). Before he was lowered into the water, Dr Harris gave Note an injection to send him to sleep, because the rescue teams did not want the boys to panic while they were underwater.

It took several hours to complete each rescue. As the divers slowly made their way through the dark waters, they held the sleeping boys close to them, for fear of knocking them against the jagged rocks.

When a diver reached a narrow section, they pulled the sleeping boy behind them in order to squeeze through.

Once they reached the dry section near the cave's entrance, the boys were strapped onto stretchers, which were each carried by a team of at least five people at a time.

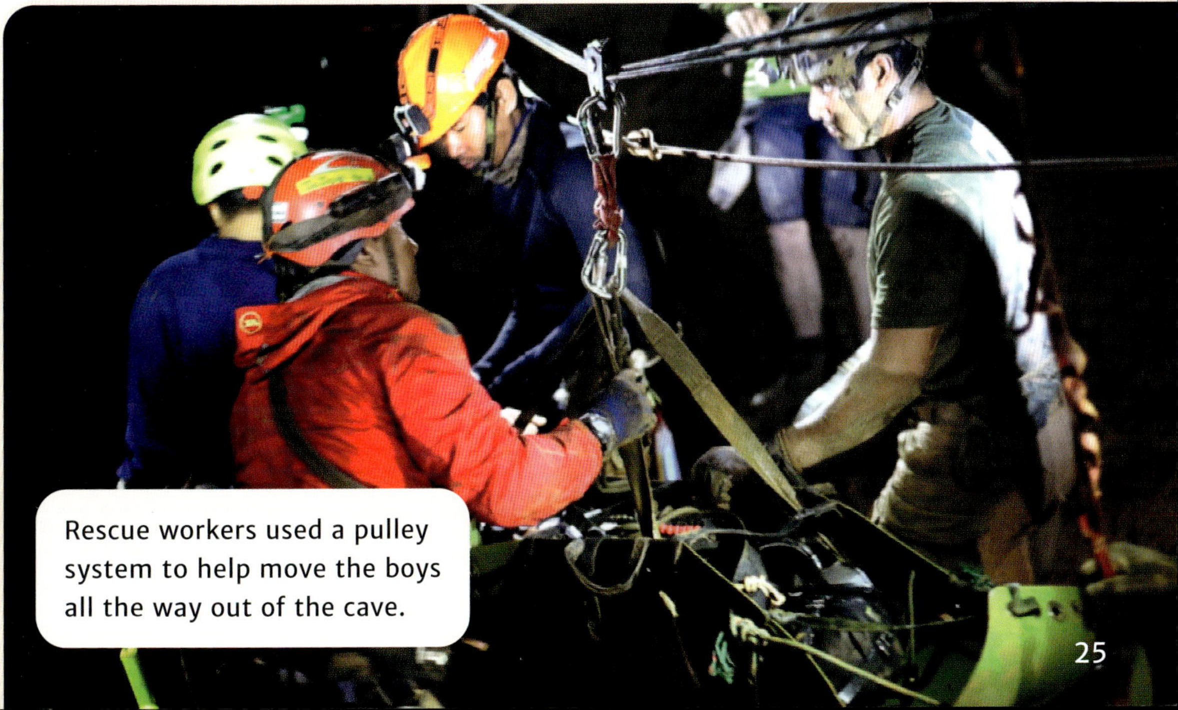

Rescue workers used a pulley system to help move the boys all the way out of the cave.

Out of the Darkness

One by one, the Wild Boars were brought out of the darkness of Tham Luang. Their families, who were waiting at the entrance, cheered and broke into tears as each boy appeared.

It took three days to rescue the entire team. Some of the divers, including the Australians, worked for 16 hours each day as they travelled back and forth through the flooded caves.

Finally, after two long weeks, the Wild Boar boys and their coach were out, safe and sound. As each boy emerged from the cave, they were given oxygen, then taken to a helicopter and flown to hospital.

Although the boys were very thin, they were all in good health.

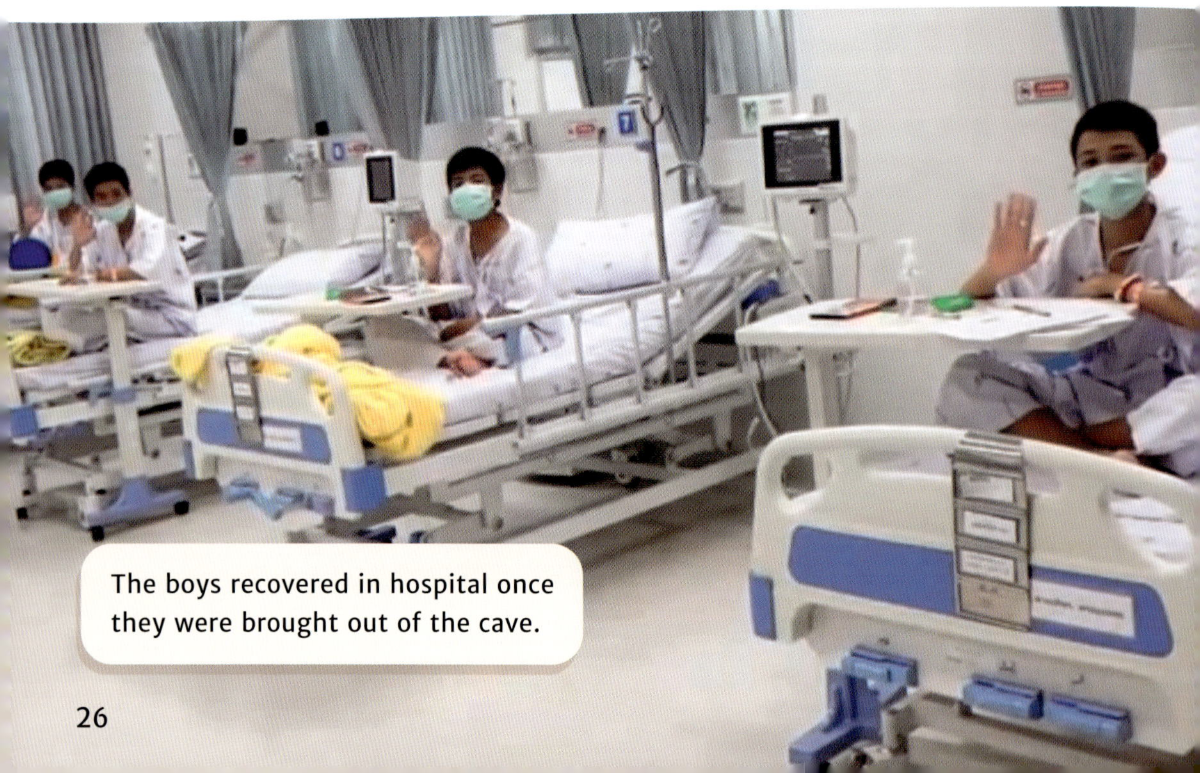

The boys recovered in hospital once they were brought out of the cave.

During their time in hospital, the boys received some sad news. One of the volunteers, a former Thai Navy SEAL, Saman Gunan, had not survived a dive through the tunnels. He had sacrificed his life to save the boys.

A bronze statue was put up at the entrance of Tham Luang to honour Saman Gunan and his sacrifice to help the Wild Boars.

To honour Saman Gunan's memory, Coach Eak and the 11 boys who were Buddhists decided to spend nine days at a Buddhist temple as **novice** monks. The boys' families believed that the meditation and prayers they learnt at the temple would give them an inner strength that would stay with them into the future.

Coach Eak (left) and 11 of the Wild Boars at the Wat Phra That Doi Tung temple

Once home, the boys returned to school. In some ways, their lives were back to normal, but in other ways, the Wild Boars had changed forever. The boys say they have become more patient and calm since their ordeal. They are also now grateful for simple things, such as a bowl of food or a hug.

In the meantime, the boys had become famous! People stopped them in the street for photos, and they were interviewed on TV. In late 2018, the boys travelled to several countries on a "thank-you tour".

The Wild Boars and their coach attended a football match in England during their "thank-you tour".

Adul Sam-on was born in Myanmar, and he moved to northern Thailand to get a better education, even though it meant leaving his family behind. He speaks several languages, which helped him to act as an **interpreter** for the English divers during the rescue.

Adul thanked the rescuers during a press conference after the boys were released from hospital.

When one of the oldest boys, Adul, was asked to speak on TV about the rescue, he said how grateful he was for the concern that people everywhere had shown. He said, "We feel like we have a lot of parents all around the world. I wish I could meet you and thank you from the bottom of my heart."

The Wild Boars had survived against all odds. Their rescue from a cave deep in the mountains was daring and dangerous, but it had succeeded.

The rescue was made possible because people from different countries, different cultures and different languages came together to achieve one common goal: to save 12 boys and their coach.

Volunteers celebrate the news that all the boys and their coach have been rescued.

The rescue effort involved more than 10 000 people, including over 100 divers, 900 police officers and 2000 soldiers.

Glossary

Buddha (*proper noun*) the founder of the religion of Buddhism

chambers (*noun*) enclosed spaces or caverns underground

Christian (*proper noun*) a person who follows the teachings of Jesus Christ

current (*noun*) strong and quick movement of water

interpreter (*noun*) a person who repeats someone's words in a different language so others can understand

monsoon season (*noun*) a period of time in some countries when heavy rains fall

novice (*noun*) a person who has only begun to learn how to do something

oxygen (*noun*) the gas in Earth's air that helps keep living things alive

sacred (*adjective*) important and highly respected within religious beliefs

scuba divers (*noun*) people who swim underwater with special gear to help them breathe

shrine (*noun*) a place to pray or make religious offerings

social media (*noun*) websites and apps that allow users to create and share content with other users

spring water (*noun*) water, usually clean, that flows up from underground

stalactites (*noun*) rocks that hang like icicles from the roof of a cave

Index